POTBELLY

ϐ in love ϐ

ORCHARD BOOKS
96 Leonard Street, London EC2A 4RH
Orchard Books Australia
14 Mars Road, Lane Cove, NSW 2066
First published in Great Britain 1996
First paperback publication 1997
The right of Rose Impey to be identified as the Author
and Keith Brumpton as the Illustrator of this Work
has been asserted by them in accordance with
the Copyright, Designs and Patents Act, 1988.
A CIP catalogue record for this book is available
from the British Library.
1 85213 894 7 (hardback)
1 86039 391 8 (paperback)
Printed in Great Britain

POTBELLY

⚘ in love ⚘

Rose Impey
keith Brumpton

ORCHARD BOOKS

POTBELLY'S RAP

Number one is Potbelly,
because he's so big.
He's brave, he's clever;
he's a popular pig.
Peewee's the smallest,
and he's number two,
Because he's Potbelly's best pal,
his right-hand shrew.
Hi-Tech Turtle has his ear
to the ground.
He's a cool dude, he's laid back,
he's wired for sound.

Potbelly ↑

ewee ↑

li-Tech

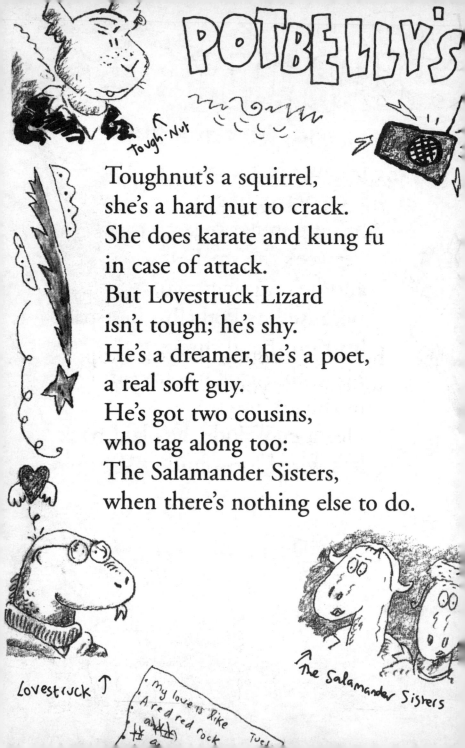

POTBELLY'S

Tough-Nut

Toughnut's a squirrel,
she's a hard nut to crack.
She does karate and kung fu
in case of attack.
But Lovestruck Lizard
isn't tough; he's shy.
He's a dreamer, he's a poet,
a real soft guy.
He's got two cousins,
who tag along too:
The Salamander Sisters,
when there's nothing else to do.

Lovestruck

The Salamander Sisters

My love is like
A red red rock

RAP

So it's business as usual,
they're all flat broke.
No money for a pizza,
a burger, or a coke.
They've nowhere to go
and nothing else to do,
but hang around the fish shop,
waiting for you.

Potbelly's dizzy.
He can't eat or drink.
He doesn't know what day it is.
He can't seem to think.

He's fallen in love
with Cherry in the shop.
Every time she serves him
his heart seems to stop.

Poor old Potbelly,
it's sad but it's true,
he's never been in love before,
he can't think what to do.

So Lovestruck tells him,
he knows what to do,
"Write her a letter, straight away,
and a poem too."

"That's great," says Peewee.
All the gang agree.
Hi-Tech says, "I'll help you, Boss,
I'm good at poetry."

They all write poems,
they write them all day.
They write a dozen each, or more,
then throw them away.

But Potbelly's finished,
he shows them his note.
The gang takes turns to read it.
This is what he wrote:

Roses are red
Bubblegum's blue
Chips smell heavenly
And so do you

← HOW ABOUT
THIS
ONE ?

From the tip of my snout
To my twirly tail
My love for you
will never fail
~~I've never seen a~~
~~girl like you before~~

From the tip of my snout
To my twirly tail
I

You are wonderful
You are the best
My love is like
an old string vest

~~My love is like an~~
~~old string vest~~

~~Shall I compare thee~~
~~To a choc-bar ?~~

CHERRY
POTBELLY

Cherry
I think you're ~~gorgus~~ gorgeous

PB

It's PB here.

"That's great," says Peewee.
Hi-Tech says, "It's ace."
The gang starts to clap and cheer,
as if he'd won a race.

But Potbelly's scared,
he's starting to shake.
The Salamander Sisters say,
"This is a mistake."

When Potbelly takes it,
he's too shy to speak.
And Snapper's waiting on the step,
he grabs it. What a cheek.

← Mr Snapper

He laughs at the poem,
chucks it in his sack.
"Go home," he says. "Get lost. Clear off.
And don't come back."

Poor old Potbelly,
it's sad but it's true,
he's never been in love before,
he can't think what to do.

So Lovestruck tells him,
"Meet her after hours.
Wait for her when she's finished work.
Take her some flowers."

"That's great," says Peewee.
"You could have asked me.
I could have told you girls like flowers."
All the gang agrees.

But Potbelly's scared,
he's starting to shake.
The Salamander Sisters say,
"This is another mistake."

They go to the fish shop.
They hang around outside.
Potbelly's standing with them,
trying not to hide.

Then out comes Cherry
with The Gopher Girls.
They hurry off the other way,
tossing back their curls.

Potbelly follows them.
They scream and run away.
Along the road comes Sergeant Snout.
It's not Potbelly's day!

Poor old Potbelly,
it's sad but it's true,
he's never been in love before,
he can't think what to do.

So Lovestruck tells him,
"Here, use Hi-Tech's phone.
Ring her up, Boss. Ask her out."
Sal and Susie groan.

"That's great," says Peewee.
Hi-Tech nods his head.
"Girls like to be taken out.
That's what my mum said."

But Potbelly's scared,
he's starting to shake.
The Salamander Sisters say,
"This is a bigger mistake."

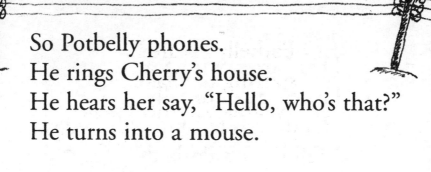

So Potbelly phones.
He rings Cherry's house.
He hears her say, "Hello, who's that?"
He turns into a mouse.

He's frozen with fear,
his legs turn to jelly.
His friends tell him what to say:
"Tell her it's Potbelly."

"Hi, Doll," they whisper.
"Ask her for a date."
"Tell her, it's that handsome pig."
"Say, Chick, I just can't wait."

It all gets mixed up.
Which one should he pick?
He says, "Hi, Pig, it's Dollybelly,
How about a chick?"

Poor old Potbelly,
it's sad but it's true,
he's never been in love before,
he can't think what to do.

So Lovestruck tells him,
"Phone Dobie, the DJ.
He'll play a record for her.
Tell him which to play."

But Potbelly's scared,
he's starting to shake.
The Salamander Sisters say,
"This is your biggest mistake."

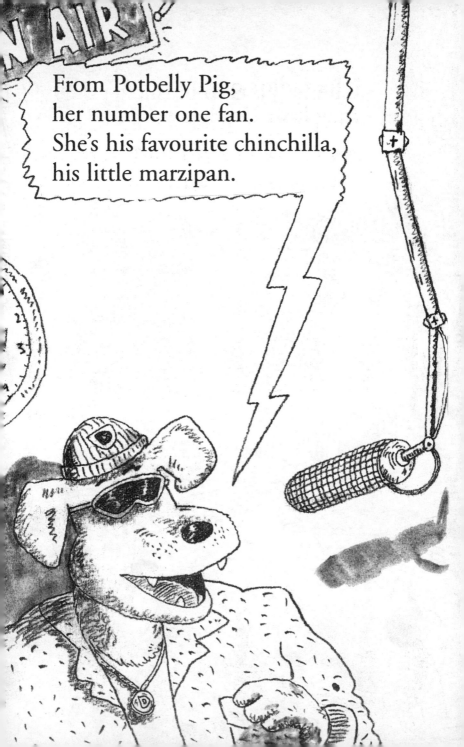

From Potbelly Pig,
her number one fan.
She's his favourite chinchilla,
his little marzipan.

Cherry starts to blush,
she rushes outside.
She's looking for Potbelly,
they almost collide.

She's holding a haddock
dripping with batter.
She slaps him round the ear with it.
His friends all scatter.

"Go away, Slop-pot,
and leave me alone.
Don't ever come round here again
and don't ever phone."

Poor old Potbelly,
he's had enough of love.
He's had enough of girls for now.
So what's he thinking of?

He's thinking of pizza
with tomatoes and peas,
olives, sweetcorn, peppers, prawns
and mozzarella cheese.

L♥VE JOKES

as told by Potbelly to PEEWEE

There was this donkey who lived in a field by the side of the river.

Oh, yes.

The donkey fell in love with a beautiful goat who lived in a field on the other side of the river.

You can read more about Potbelly
in these other books...

Potbelly and the Haunted House

185213 891 2 (hb)   1 86039 388 8 (pb)

Potbelly's Lost His Bike

1 85213 892 0 (hb)   1 86039 389 6 (pb)

Potbelly Needs a Job

1 85213 893 9 (hb)   1 8 6039 390 X (pb)